North Pole

Arctic Ocean

Dear Reader,

I am proud to partner with Kohl's Cares and introduce young readers to Penguin and Bear. Each book features a universal theme that tugs at our hearts—such as losing and finding a favorite stuffed animal, feeling safe on a stormy night, making new (and sometimes unexpected!) friends on vacation, and the wonder of learning about new things. My hope is that when you share these books with the children in your life, they will feel as if they've just been given a warm hug and be inspired to discover more about the world around them.

I am passionate about childhood literacy and learning, and I am thrilled that Kohl's shares in this passion. Thank you for supporting Kohl's Cares and a lifelong love of reading for children everywhere!

Your friend,

Salina Yoon

Indian Ocean

Antarctica

For Mike and Elim

First published in the United States of America in September 2015
by Bloomsbury Children's Books
www.bloomsbury.com

Bloomsbury is a registered trademark of Bloomsbury Publishing Plc

For information about permission to reproduce selections from this book, write to
Permissions, Bloomsbury Children's Books, 1385 Broadway, New York, New York 10018
Bloomsbury books may be purchased for business or promotional use. For information on bulk purchases
please contact Macmillan Corporate and Premium Sales Department at specialmarkets@macmillan.com

Library of Congress Cataloging-in-Publication Data
Yoon, Salina, author, illustrator.
Penguin's big adventure / by Salina Yoon.
pages   cm
Summary: Penguin embarks on his next journey—becoming the first penguin to explore the North Pole! Along the way, he says hello to all his old
friends. But when he finally reaches his destination, he realizes he's all alone in a strange, foreign place. How will Penguin overcome his fears of the
unknown and enjoy this new adventure?
ISBN 978-0-8027-3828-8 (hardcover) • ISBN 978-1-61963-730-6 (board book)
ISBN 978-0-8027-3830-1 (e-book) • ISBN 978-0-8027-3831-8 (e-PDF)
[1. Penguins—Fiction. 2. Animals—Fiction. 3. Adventure and adventurers—Fiction. 4. Voyages and travels—Fiction.
5. North Pole—Fiction. 6. Friendship—Fiction.] I. Title.
PZ7.Y817Ph 2015   [E]—dc23   2014047140

ISBN 978-1-68119-171-3 (Kohl's)

Art created digitally using Adobe Photoshop • Typeset in Maiandra • Book design by Nicole Gastonguay
Printed in China by RR Donnelley Asia, Dongguan City, Guangdong
1 3 5 7 9 10 8 6 4 2

Kohl's
Style: 1681191717
Factory Number: 123386
2/16–3/16

This special edition was printed for Kohl's Department Stores, Inc.
(for distribution on behalf of Kohl's Cares, LLC, its wholly owned subsidiary)
by Bloomsbury Children's Books.

Penguin's Big Adventure

Penguin was here!

Salina Yoon

BLOOMSBURY

NEW YORK LONDON OXFORD NEW DELHI SYDNEY

One day, Penguin had a big idea.

He wanted to do something no penguin had ever done.

He wanted to be the first penguin ever to set foot on the North Pole.

Penguin planned and packed.
He rolled up his adventure map
and set off.

But before his first mile,
Penguin saw Emily sewing.

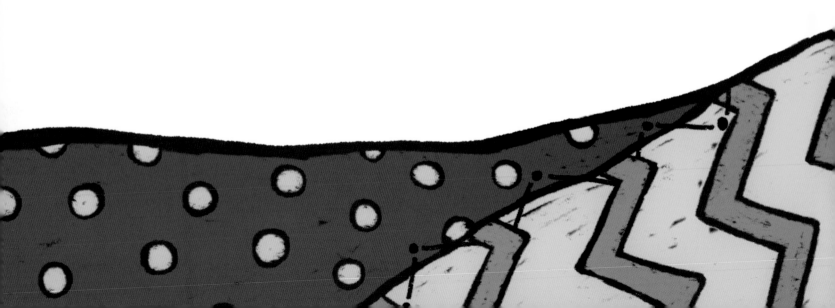

"This looks like a very nice quilt," said Penguin, "and the brightest I've ever seen!"

Before Penguin reached his second mile, he saw his little brother, Pumpkin, weaving.

"That is a fine basket, Pumpkin!" said Penguin, "and the biggest I've ever seen!"

Right before his third mile, he saw Bootsy braiding the longest rope he'd ever seen.

Then Penguin set off for the other side of the world, while his busy friends worked on their own world records.

Penguin passed through his favorite places and visited with old friends.

He had a whale of a time!

Finally, Penguin reached the North Pole.

Penguin threw confetti,

turned cartwheels,

Penguin
was here!

and planted a sign.

Penguin shouted, "HOORAY!"
and it echoed across the ice.

Nobody answered.

Penguin was suddenly lonely and afraid.

But he was not alone.

Penguin had never
seen a polar bear.

And Polar Bear had never seen a penguin.

It was scary.

Penguin and Polar Bear smiled.
And it wasn't so scary anymore.

Do you wear a black belt?

No, I wear an orange scarf!

Do you have big, sharp teeth?

No, but one might be coming in!

Together they went on a North Pole adventure.

They went whale watching,

built ice forts,

explored the Arctic Sea,

and welcomed
more visitors!

Then it was time for the
new friends to say good-bye.

Penguin left Polar Bear his adventure map. He didn't need it anymore.

Because the best part of
having an adventure is . . .

World Record

First penguin to set foot on the North Pole!

Penguin

Certified by **Grandpa**

Witnessed by **Polar Bear**

World Record

First polar
bear to meet
a penguin!

Polar Bear
_____

Certified by _____Grandpa_____

Witnessed by _____Penguin_____

Arctic Ocean
North America
Pacific Ocean
Atlantic Ocean
South America
N
W
E
S